Meicke, the Devil

Meicke, the Devil

Hermann Stehr

K A Nitz
Albany, New Zealand

Meicke, der Teufel published
in *Auf Leben und Tod* 1898

The Inspektor first published in *Schlesisches Dichterbuch* (edited by August Krause) 1902

Mein Leben first published 1922
as "Ein Erinnerungsblatt" in *Mit Gerhart Hauptmann: Erinnerungen und Bekenntnisse aus seinem Freundeskreis* (edited by Walter Heynen).

Revised printing October 2019

ISBN: 978-0-473-21362-6

National Library of New Zealand Cataloguing-in-Publication Data

Stehr, Hermann, 1864-1940.
Meicke, der Teufel. English
Meicke, the Devil / by Hermann Stehr ;
translated by Kerry Nitz.
ISBN 978-0-473-21362-6
l. Nitz, Kerry, 1971- ll. Title
833.912—dc 22

Contents

Meicke, the Devil...............................7

The Inspector...................................91

An Excerpt from *My Life*...............121

Meicke, the Devil

The mountains stood all around, blue-black, like they always are in spring. The sky lay above them, dark and dismal. Only a red streak was swimming over the peaks and gradually losing itself in the high air, in strips and smoky haze.

In the middle of the land ... it swung into hills, it stumbled into valleys and ravines, it thrust upwards in broad, massive high ridges to the blue-black mountains and the hazy red strips over them ... in the middle of the land, between the cities, in the open country which stretched out in the nakedness of its brown fields, there he sat on the edge of the ditch, raking his beard with his grubby right hand and then wiping onto this legs the spittle from the corners of his mouth.

The main road ran off to his right and it ran off to his left, straight as a drawbar. But here, like there, it turned from its course with a kick. At each bend a cross stood. And both saviours looked each other in the face. They looked at each other, musing with the mild air of brooding wisdom.

The figures of the saviour are not dead. They can move and have powers. Sometimes, at night, they come to life. Then they climb down from their crucifix, stretch their arms and stroll across the fields. With the first rooster's cry they return again to their agony between heaven and earth.

The field obtains its crops, the sky the rain and good wind, and the road its security from these quiet walks which only sunday children can see. That's also why only sinful wagoners crack their whips in front of a cross. The good ones, however, clean their right thumb on their trousers, make a cross with it, travel past and, when they are well past, whistle because they know that now bad luck does not have any hold over them anymore.

Wenzel had also acted like the good wagoners. He is now sitting between both the saviours and waiting for something to happen.

The saviour on the right ponders and does nothing.

The saviour on the left ponders and hesitates.

Finally it takes too long for Wenzel.

He strikes his knee with the palm of his hand encouragingly and looks at the crosses, one after the other, timidly but for a long time.

The dog on the road in front of the two-wheeled sand cart springs up at the sound and looks at his master through overhanging brows.

"Lie down, Meicke, they never think of others like they do with us."

Meicke throws a testing look at the cart, rolls the whites of his eyes back and forth, then lies down again, shoves his muzzle under his hind leg and goes to sleep.

Girrack! Girrack!

From the field's derelict irrigation ditch whirs the mating call of a partridge.

In the distance there are three black patches on the field, stands of trees. In the whitish haze of the expanse a church tower leans in boredom.

Wenzel yawns.

After that he clears his throat impatiently. But nothing happens, and he lapses into thought, ... it was a long time ago. — —

The doctors at the hospital in Lemburg let him go, as they maintained he was healthy, quite healthy. But he angrily stamped his crookedly healed leg on the ground. It was meant to say, do you call that healthy?

He shrugged his shoulders. In the end it did not change anything for the board cutters. Why did they let the klutz walk on the leg? Nothing doing there.

He looked at them full of hate for a long time, until his eyeballs burned, then swore loudly and walked hurriedly to a tavern. There he bought himself schnaps.

After that he got plucky and crossed the German border. But when the money was gone his pluck stopped too. He fell, senseless for enfeeblement, in a ditch by the roadside.

When he awoke, a large piece of black bread lay next to his head, and a black, ugly dog sat at his feet. Its hair was bristly, long, and in some places caked by mud into clumps. A prickly moustache stood on its upper lip so that its muzzle seemed even plumper than it would otherwise be. Its forelegs were turned outwards at the elbows.

"Actually it's shit that I've woken up", was the first thought that clearly entered Wenzel's head.

But the dog was looking at him so mildly with its large, brown eyes.

That's why he forgave himself his reawakening, sat down on the verge and began to eat the bread which some sympathetic hand had placed next to him. That took quite a while, as owing to fatigue and low spirits he was only capable of moving his lower jaw with some effort.

He chewed on the bread until he was tired.

Then he called to the ugly animal which had been sitting there without stirring until then.

The dog came slowly, cowering, timid. After a long hesitation it took the proffered bread cautiously with its lips. With that it wagged its tail gratefully.

Wenzel pondered, "The dog is like you. Only you have a home and it ... it ... who does it have? — Who knows, perhaps it is completely wild ... but its eyes, its brown, expressive eyes."

Then a wagon went past. Two drunken farmers were sitting on it. One of them was cracking the whip, the other was swearing and singing. The former looked over to him and called out, "Little brother, what are you feeding the devil?"

In fact, that had not yet occurred to him. The devil sometimes comes in the form of a dog.

But why would the devil take the trouble? His soul belonged to him anyway.

Perhaps, however, it is better anyway! — — And he looked for somewhere he could chase the dog to.

In the direction his eyes took, thatched rooves were peering out from the trees' greenery.

The dog was from there, his home was there. So he did not need to chase the brute away.

For — why, he did not know — he felt that he could not strike the dog.

That's why he stood up and went.

In the village the dog would surely lose itself.

But, when he had the houses at his back and looked around, he noticed that the dog was still trotting behind him, its head bowed, and its claws crunching on the stones.

Wenzel screamed and hit the ground with his stick to scare it away. But all his efforts had no result other than to make the dog spring into the meadow, sit down there and whimper gently.

That made him feel bad, and because he remembered that he actually had no one in the whole wide world, he called the mutt over to pat it.

But it did not come to him anymore.

Alone, as Wenzel strode on again, the dog followed him from a distance.

Finally he arrived on the ridge of a small hill.

Below, far off on the plain, a river was meandering. A man was walking back and forth by it. Something bright as silver flashed above his head. A border guard!

Over there, across the misty water, far off, lay his home, a new life.

There I'll sleep again like I should — why not even in a bed?! — —

Two boys came running over the hill, a large, dark-haired boy in front and a small, blonde-haired boy behind him. The latter had a big piece of bread in his hand and was screaming because he could not catch the bigger boy.

The boys' eyes sparkled, their cheeks glowed; they were so fleet of foot! Their bare feet slapped hurriedly on the path.

... they were past.

If a life could run like that, uphill, with laughing eyes and plump cheeks! — —

Suddenly a desperate cry screams from a child's mouth behind him.

His head turns around abruptly.

The blonde, rotund little boy lies there on the path. The black, bristly dog is standing over him and baring its teeth.

The child is lost! — The dog is wild!

"Dammit! ... shoo! ... Mongrel!" —

The beast lets off and ambles unhurriedly to the ditch, the little one's bread in its fangs.

The youth has sprung up and is running to the larger boy, who, paralysed with terror, had been watching the incident from a distance. Now they fling their arms around each other, then turn around and shout at the dog, "Meicke!"

What is it, its name or a swearword?

Devil — — — Meicke ...

Shaking his head, Wenzel turns around.

The river shimmers in the distance. It glistens through the white haze and curls in the many colours of high summer.

His home ... a new life! — Truly, a new life! — Curse the schnaps, the people, the game ... this time, this time it'll be different.

If only he were already across that great water! Cautiously, using every fold in the ground, he creeps down to the bushes on the banks, the dog behind him at a distance, but persistently following.

After a gruelling hour, he arrives down below, lies down in a thick stand of hazel and goes to sleep.

He awakes in the night.

The river is roaring louder.

The stars are flashing sharply, many thousands of them.

Yes, why am I here, the words flare up in him in fearful curiosity, and what is that roaring?

He turns his head and looks musingly into the tangle of black trunks and stems around him.

Satan! — like burning phosphorous in the darkness, two blue-green points, motionless next to each other! —

Meicke! — — Meicke! — —

A soft, weak whimpering answers.

The grass rustles, slumbering.

The luminous points come closer, swaying fitfully.

Finally a cold nose thrusts itself into his hand.

"Poor hussy, so you're called Meicke! But we'll soon have to part from each other. For a change, as it happens, I won't need a devil."

But he takes the bristly head between his hands anyway and squeezes it affectionately, and warmth wells up in him.

"Adieu, Meicke!" — —

Then he pushes it away with his foot.

After that he stands up, peers keenly to all sides, shuffles forward, listens, creeps further, going slowly from trunk to trunk.

On such a border the lead shot often sits looser in its barrel, accursedly.

So!

Not because of his current life, but his new life! He would lose it and die with a taste in his mouth, dull as shit.

There! — — — — the water trundles by his feet.

Above all, he instills in himself once more, while he binds his coat tightly with a cord to his back, above all breathe calmly, a calm rhythm. The rest is in God's hands ... the water splashes over him.

All goes well.

When the sun appears, he is sitting naked, huddled up, in the thick bushes. On the branches his wet clothes are flapping in the warm light.

He has nothing but the breath in his lungs and the hope in his soul.

But he is so happy, so light.

The struggle with the waters was his baptism cleansing him of guilt.

Around him, across the fields, the warmth of the day is taking affect and the air is trembling in it.

He stares with a fixed shining gaze into the glow for a long time.

Black balls are already dancing before his gaze, but he does not turn away. It is so beautiful looking into the light.

The balls revolve in circles. As he moves his eyes they dance.

No, but not ...

One is running along the ground to him.

He raises his eyes up, high—er — high—er.

The black ball is run—ning to him.

Hand over the eyes! ... oh! ... yes it is ... through the water? ... Nonsense! ... it's all no use, Meicke, the devil from Galicia. — —

Its nose close to the ground, it runs up to him wagging its stumpy tail.

With a joyful cry he rushes up to it. Starved, abandoned, stinking, it attaches itself to his feet.

The cast out life awakens in him again and lies over his hopes the way miscreants lie down on flowers.

It chills him — — a gulp of schnaps!

He carefully draws his clothes in. Then he cuts himself a stick and strikes out for the village which lies over there in the midst of the fields.

There he goes from door to door. He is given bread and money.

The bread he shares with Meicke. With the money he buys schnaps.

And when he is lying drunk in the stable that evening, his hope visits him. He looks at it and cries, and his tears stream into the manure in which he is lying.

In the morning his turbid life sinks over him again and dulls him.

Meicke does not shy from him anymore.

Thus at the start of winter he reaches his home, poor Rutersdorf, having spent half a year in his wandering. His brother hosts him in the lean-to next to the ramshackle sitting room, the only room in the cottage. His brother is older. He does not wake anymore from his sad, wretched life.

In summer, they ply sand. In winter, they bind brooms with switchs they steal.

It is enough for potatoes, bread and coffee.

Sometimes a groschen is left over. Then they both have some fun. They get drunk, the brother from weakness, in a frenzy which throws into his depraved head the words fortune and relief — which then go around in it like a paroxysm. —

The strain of desire drives him to it. For hope has become invisible in him. It lies in him, a burning, an unease, a listlessness, like saliva on the tongue that he cannot get rid of. But when drunk it stands up and becomes as big as it ever was, tangible, visible, laughs at him, whips and stings.

Then he lies in his lean-to on the rags, biting his own hand until it bleeds. He strikes out furiously, swears despairingly, all because he loves his hope, but knows that in the morning it will have flown away into the bleak grey of his helplessly wretched life. All that the sun leaves him is a restless, ever aimless brooding for a way out. He finds hundreds, thousands, countless. But just for that reason everything is pointless.

For a long time, he fumbled in waning desire like this. But he still came up with nothing other than the despairing look in his eye.

Now he is again standing in front of the insurmountable wall with the ant-like whirl of dancing hollow thoughts, as always — and he sees his misery so tangibly around himself that he lifts his heavy, lowered head up. With one eye wandering around, he asks the whole world as it were, in his inept helplessness, for help.

But his consciousness suddenly springs from the train of turbid memories. It is a waste to be sitting so lost.

For today, on this spring morning, a miracle has happened to him. In complete sobriety hope has awoken in him.

All miracles come from above, from the being which he knelt before as an innocent boy.

That's also why he is sitting in the midst of the fields, between the towns, under the gentle sky. On the right a saviour, on the left a saviour. They will finally help him. But ... the blue mountains sleep for the longest time behind the evening haze! In the motionless air the sound of bells tolling fades away. Then there is a roaring over by the three patches of forest ... a train, or the forest is sleeping. —

"Then why don't you ever help me? — Are you never the saviour? — — — because I'm a rogue? — Do the good need a saviour then?" — —

A certainty rises in him cold and slow. The world has forgotten him, heaven too. But Wenzel doesn't crumble. Defiantly, wildly, he snatches in the grass ... he spits in the air ... ha, ha! — a contemptuous laughter.

"Now it's over! If I want to have it different then I have to do it different. — The rest is silliness and gossip. And I will!", he concluded with threatening earnesty.

"Meicke!"

The cart creaked.

Wenzel felt his way to it.

"Are you there?! — If you are gone, my troubles will break me too. Truly, Meicke means devil, I see now."

He unyoked the dog and took its harness off. Then he grabbed it by the scruff of its neck. In his heart a tremor probably awoke, but he swallowed it.

Did he want to feel sympathy for his dreary life? — No! — Already merciless blows were swishing over the dog's back. It cried with pain, it wreathed in his hand. Wenzel noticed nothing, he was senseless with rage and pity. Finally the animal managed to loose itself. Whimpering it fled across the road into the field. Wenzel ran swearing after it. He ran, with gasping chest and threatening words, until he was exhausted. After fighting for his breath, he finally stood still and listened out into the night.

All is calm. —

Now he had chased away his weakness and his vices. In no way would they find their way back to him. But the cart also had to go, so nothing would remind him of his past anymore.

With effort he found his way back to the place in which he had been sitting. The cart still stood there. He gripped it by the drawbar and smashed it into a wreck on the road. He stomped the spokes out of the wheels.

Then he contentedly went on his way.

When he came to the cross that had stood to his left, he dugs his hands deeper in his pockets, looked the other way and laughed scornfully, "God! — wood and nails, nothing else!" —

The next morning, he came to an end with his brooding.

He knew exactly what he had to do, rose in his lean-to, peered with one eye through a crack in the wall, and then called out into the room,

"Seff!"

"What."

"I'm going soon."

"Then go!"

"But I'm never coming back."

"So ... oh ..."

The burnt out, hollow man's voice quavered for a while in astonishment, then rattled into a falsetto and concluded, "... an ape!"

It seemed unthinkable. Once someone was in this lean-to, they also had to perish in it. But Wenzel knew exactly what he had to do. He placed fifteen greasy nickels, his entire savings, on the bench by the wall.

"My money is lying on the bench."

"Money! — Money!" his brother called blissfully from inside the sitting room. "You're going in God's name too, good man!"

Indeed, he was going too.

The plum trees hung full of drops. He walked stooped beneath them and soon stood on the road in the full glow of the rising sun. He looked into its young fervour and an image from his childhood surrounded this prospect. It was the only one in which the magic of the morning of his life spoke to him. He had forgotten the other days which had passed with downcast eyes, hungry and ragged. This one image contained his entire childhood.

Now in the shimmer of the rising sun it was coming to life in him again.

— — — — — — He was full from beggar's bread and making eyes like a contented child. The grass in which he was sitting was green, radiant green. The leaves slept above him in the trees, and it was as though they were dreaming something very beautiful, for the little cheeks of their white leaves burned with fervour. The birds were singing their gentle songs, and the light hummed along inexpressibly blissful. But he was stroking the grass, which was soft, soft as human hair. And a little round beetle ran over his little hand. He raised his hand slowly, for it was red and had black spots.

"Fly, ladybird! — Fly ladybird!"

The round beetle ran busily up and down on the splayed fingers of his raised hand, and when it arrived at the tip of his golden finger it nodded cheerfully a few times with its little black head, sedately raised its glass wings under their covers and flew away, far, far away into Pomerania. The little beetle was flying in front of him again today and sat down on the roof of a gardener's hut in the forest.

His new life resided in this house.

He met a girl in front of the door. She was tall and skinny. Her full mouth was always open.

In it stood long, whitish-yellow teeth. The big aquamarine eyes wandered about as though lost.

"How old are you, little Marie?"

"Fifteen years old."

"Soo! — fif—teen — years — hm, hm", and he eyed her up for a while, and with the index finger of his right hand he wiped the corner of his mouth musingly. "Fif—teen — years —" he repeated thoughtfully.

Marie turned red under the man's searching look, and turned her back to him.

"Where is your mother then?"

"Inside", the child answered over her shoulder.

***

"Nice girl, Stumpy!"

"Good morning! Well, what brings you?" The woman had served in a guest house for a few years in her youth and, as a result, was speaking a city dialect.

"Good water, and me."

"Good water, yes, but you? — to me?"

"Because it isn't evening."

"I don't need a man here at all anymore. Who, who said that, hey?" She stepped threateningly up to the man.

"The little Marie."

"The! ..."

"Yes, and her father, old Kliegel, who breathed his last in the hospital after you broke his business." —

"I broke his business? He left his child, little Marie, behind."

"His, *his* child? Calm down. Stumpy, I've had it for days in the chest, and when I laugh, it hurts", and after he had looked at her with a malicious smile for some time, he continued scornfully, "Yes, and why did that good father have to, since the house had a lien on it, why did he have to end up in a hospital like a sardine tin?" —

"Because he had a contagious disease."

"Stop, stop, Stumpy, it's tearing me up!" And he broke out into forced, screaming laughter, holding his sides.

"Wenzel, Wenzel! What an animal! There's no room in my house for a rogue!"

"Or for a whore."

"Me?"

"Ah my whore! — — No, Stumpy, I have never forgotten the nights in there. More than twenty times I went through that window, me and others."

"You ... but others ..."

"I know them all! — What have I to lose? But you! I want the sparrows to learn to sing that song about you until they drive you out of the village."

The lips of the short, skinny woman flew and her eyes blazed. Then she laughed keenly and fawning, and looked at Wenzel from the side.

He raised himself from the table and stepped up to her.

"Here, feel my arm, here, my leg. What do you think? They are hard from work and ready for anything."

The lust emaciated woman pondered for a moment. Then she asked stealthily, "Who sent you here?" —

"My misery."

"What has your misery got to do with me?"

"You? Do you think I still have money like your old Kliegel! Money for you, that you'll still spit at me, when it's gone?"

The woman walked hesitantly into the next room.

After a while she returned and laid a taler on the table.

"Here, take it and go and leave me in peace."

Wenzel shook his head in silence.

The woman laid another taler down, then another, then another, hesitantly and dickering as though it involved a business that she had been striving to turn to her advantage through as much tenacity as possible.

Wenzel laughed purposefully.

Then a hot fury took possession of the woman. She grasped the broom by the hearth, raised it, and screamed, "Now out, out immediately, or this broom will pelt your skull till you lose your senses. Ha! no, you won't chase my business, my hard earned business, down your throat. No, not unless it's over my dead body!"

But smiling coldly, Wenzel grasped her by the wrist and turned it so the broom dropped from her hand.

Pale, shaking, the woman looked at him with hate filled eyes. In vain she sought to free the hand sitting in the man's vice-like grasp.

A deep silence unfolded.

Then Wenzel took a deep breath, and the expression on his face changed. He began again, and his voice sounded truthful, endearing, and urgent, "Come, childish woman! You keep your money. I don't want any crumbs from the field, timber from

the wood, or wool from the sheep. I'm neither hungry nor thirsty. But I still have hunger and thirst for a different life. I had to get out of that lean-to or stay in rags. Meicke is gone, the cart lies smashed on the road. — Now I stand before you. Take me in. I want to be your lad. I will work for two and I won't ask for anything. I'll be happy with whatever you give me. Kathrine, come, give me your hand of your own will."
—

A hesitant silence occurred. The guardian angel of human vice flew through the room and smiled. Its fervent breath skimmed over the woman's lost soul and the old addiction awoke in it.

"Friend, you think I'm still young. No, because of that it isn't necessary anymore, because of that I won't marry."

You shouldn't have to. Hate me as you will, I'll be your shepherd, your worker, your employee." And after slow pondering the words came spontaneously from the depths of his furthest thoughts, "What should have been, will be."

The woman related that to herself and smiled.

Wenzel hung his jacket on the post by the hearth, "Where's the scythe?"

"It's hanging in the house."

Thereupon he left the room, walked into the meadow, and started scything.

The woman made the morning coffee, and placed three little pots on the table.

After that the three ate together.

So began Wenzel's new life.

He would not, as a boy, have let the little beetle fly off otherwise.

Diligence now erupted passionately like a mania from Wenzel's head, from his body. It exhausted him in summer's fervour. It froze him in the frost of the forest as he gathered wood. It drove him down the road selling berries, threw him from limb to limb. But his strength seemed inexhaustible in stamina, his head full of tricks and wiles.

The woman watched him with admiration and pride as he soldiered on. She had truly made a good deal with him.

The wheat waved in the field. The money piled up in the drawer of the chest.

He never spoke of marrying, never of reward. He never slurred "Good evening!", even if he came home quite late.

Once she secretly placed a bottle of schnaps next to his bed. On the next morning the bottle together with its contents had disappeared. Then she became afraid, and she looked at him scornfully with blazing eyes. But he chirruped, "Haha, come!", taking a shovel and going with her into the garden. Under a tree the lawn was wilted. There he struck the shovel into the ground and lifted out the bottle.

"Missing a drop of it?"

"No, never! But why did you bury it?"

"Just like my alcoholism."

He shook the bottle. The schnaps splashed against the glass as if it were laughing and it sparkled.

Then Wenzel closed his eyes and hurled it against a trunk so that it smashed noisily.

It was to him as though something had called him, and he walked over and smashed the pieces to dust so that whatever spirit in it that had called him was dead.

After that the fervour grew in the woman, and with longing arms she was grasping after his body.

Don't just watch the years, there's no point in that. But swing on them, they'll come to you meek as a lamb on the lead of your plans. As the rider, so the horse.

Wenzel was a strong, reckless, unrelenting rider. He finally trotted through the bedchamber of Kathrine Stumpf, went down into the yard, looked along the building and said, "My little business is the tops."

Since he saw Kathrine Stumpf at the window, he called to her gruffly, "Kathrine, let the cow out."

The woman appeared quickly at the front door, but she stumbled abruptly in the process, bit her lip angrily, shook her head, placed her hands on her hips and replied razor-sharp, "What did you say? — Kathrine?" —

You could see she was fighting it inwardly and did it anyway. The chains rattled in the barn, with swinging tails the chaste cows skipped into the yard. Kathrine Stumpf, however, flung the bolt furiously so it skipped clinking over the cobbles. She had found her tamer. With deft skill he ruled her through her body.

He smiled condescendingly. She, however, was longing for him with oaths and profanities. *She* was still master,

"My cows are like girls!" —

"Yes, yes, our cows are the nicest by far."

"Our? — our — mine and little Marie's, yes, ours!"

Wenzel just laughed. Then he spoke firmly and clearly, "I have sold the deer to the butcher by weight. They'll fetch eight talers."

Kathrine Stumpf erupted in fierce scolding.

He shrugged his shoulders nonchalantly, said, "It's done", and walked away whistling.

Night after night now, he strode laughing into her bedroom.

On the fourth night, just as he was climbing the steps to his room, Kathrine Stumpf appeared on the threshold.

"Are you going up to sleep, dear?"

"Yes!"

"Your bed will never be the warmest."

"I like it, I make a lot of heat."

"Sleep well."

"You too."

The door flew shut with a bang. The woman stood behind it and shook her fists at the man,

"Oh you ... you! — such a ... oh!"

But Wenzel blithely kept climbing, lay a while on his bed with open eyes, his hands shoved under his head, then spat and went to sleep. Then, on the seventh night, he was looking at the forest through his open window.

A heavy darkness lay outside. A humid wind burrowed into the haystacks, as it was June.

The tallow candle on the table glowed red and a long plume towered over the puny little flame.

Wenzel leant snugly against the wall as he waited with half-open eyes for sleep to come.

Marie sat on a stool and looked with bashful, dejected face at her hands folded in her lap.

Kathrine Stumpf was pale. Her gaunt face was labouring. She played on the table with her cold hand. She warred with herself, alone in vain.

"Little Marie, go to sleep", she said then with beating chest, and did not dare look at her daughter.

She crept out, almost fainting from the shuddering of her shame. Up above, her daughter buried herself in bed, and cried until her trembling soul came to rest in sleep.

In the room below it remained deadstill.

Wenzel's eyelids were sinking further over his lingering eyes.

Kathrine Stumpf had become paler.

She glanced with hostility into the fluctuating sparks of light, and absorbed in deep draughts the humid, gently burrowing fervour which was coming in through the open window.

Then she put the light out with an abrupt snatch, and stammered into the darkness with dry, heavy tongue, "Why aren't I good enough for you anymore? — — Sell the deer — — do what you will — — — — — but — I — — I —", the searching arms entwined the still motionless woman.

"What are you bridling at now?", countered the victor, and took her in his arms.

You know it too — — — — — — — — — The earth is staring with blunt contours into the air.

It is lying motionless, as if it were frightened of ghosts and hardly dares to breath. Only its water throbs fearfully through the night.

The sky, its mother, its father ...

It is bending mute over the earth and watching with its deep, loving star-eyes at the child that cannot sleep, cloaking it in soft, grey pillows of night mist and stroking them smooth. Then a soft, dreamlike breeze picks up. You do not feel it on the cheeks, not once in the eye, you only notice it in the drowsy stirring of the lowered, tired leaves of the tree. This stroking of the grieved mother's hand also went over the body of the earth on that night when the ardency awoke in them both.

They lay next to each other in bed, and the blue-white light of the night came in soundlessly through the open window, and when it saw them both it trembled and fled outside again.

But it came back in again, curious, and went out shaking and told it to all the light outside whose chastity lay over the sleeping earth. And soon all the light was trembling around their bed.

The man's soul looked inwards with large, burning eyes.

The woman's soul peered through the timorous opening of quaking lids.

Thus the ardency awoke in them both. And it knelt before the woman's soul and asked her tearfully with the chaste eyes of a child, with the hands on which there was no trace of burden yet, "Oh mother, mother!"

Then Kathrine Stumpf sat up, silently, gingerly, slowly. Her bare, sharp-edged arms sank slack and cold onto the covers.

Under her lowered brow, her eyes were glowing. They were becoming perceptive. —

She looked at what her ardency had created. For it had grown and gone out from her soul into her life and had pulled aside the veil, the red, gleaming veil of her lust.

Thus the woman saw for the first time with her eyes, for the first time in forty five years.

There it lay before her, in the trembling, blue-white light of the night — a morass growing endlessly in breadth, languid, stinking water lying in the fields, drowning the crops at their peak; towns under construction brought to ruin ... this morass flowed from a light, sweet like the sunshine in early May, and disappeared outside in a strip of land where the childish bright fervour of the sun was skipping around buds which drank the light and blossomed in it.

The woman saw the morass and dared not say anything for awe.

He saw the sweet light of his beginning, and sighed, "Ah, once more, to be a child just one last time!" —

She saw the distant land, "Little Marie, my poor girl."

When the woman saw it, she sank with her face against the wall and cried. She didn't cry timorously into her hands, no, she sobbed loudly and bitterly.

But, in Wenzel, the ardency arose differently when he looked into the light. His soul was torn open, tempestuously as though on fire, and his hope had erupted into flames. It looked wildly around his inner being, scornful, laughing, "Ha, ha! Old man! Bon appetit! haha." —

It was gone.

He sucked on the night with his burning eyes. But the runaway did not return anymore.

Only its scornful, fiercely bitter laughter had remained, "Haha!" —

It struck like the lash of a whip across his soul, so that he was writhing under it in fury and rage. That's why he swore to himself, "Good, finally, dammit, finally!" —

The woman next to him, however, was crying, fitfully, dull, ceaselessly.

Finally he could no longer stand it.

"What are you bawling for — ha, Stumpy?!" —

"I'm sick, sick ... Wenzel."

"Should I go perhaps?"

"Yes, until you're asked for and ... and ...", but she didn't blurt out what she wanted to say, as her anguish, the shattering image of her ardency, had softly disappeared, and the gleaming, red veil was slowly flowing over her entire being again.

She stretched her hands out into the darkness, caught the man's arm and squeezed it fervently.

Digging into Wenzel's breast, however, was his hope's lashing laughter.

He squeezed the woman roughly to himself, and felt his way to his room.

But the woman fell asleep. Actually it was not sleep at all.

A grey, dreary haze came over the escaping images of her inner being. She lay as though under a spell, as though spun around by dream-like shackles. Her thoughts were leaking out and coalescing in strange patterns — people turned into houses that could walk, flocks of birds turned into forests which sang. She absorbed the scent of these phantasmal transformations with weary, weary lust, and it was to her as though her body was being rocked by waves, without a push, without being nudged, gently, softly.

And look, there was an ocean above her, an ocean below her. Light was between them, a gentle, timorous light like that made at dusk when the night's inert blue flows into the expiring red fervour of evening.

She was hanging or lying in this light whose horizon grew shimmering all around into eternity, and she listened to the lulling murmur of the oceans above and below her.

Suddenly a thunderclap broke from the ocean above her, a hard, physical rumble. The timorous light in which she was lying or hanging trembled the way the light swells when a hanging lamp is pushed by the wind.

Then the sound ran with fleeing steps into the ocean below her, and a door in it, which she had not seen at all up to then, flew open, screeching and wheezing. A girl plunged through it into the light — her black hair unfastened, her body bent forward in flight, convulsed by fear, her arms reddened from struggling, and in a shirt which slipped half over her shoulder. Every extremity was a solitary, gripping scream for help. But the haunted girl's pondering, deep-pitying, praying eyes were restraining her mouth, which wanted to speak, so that only her lips curved in sympathy. A frisson convulsed her. Silently she raised her arms in the air and sank slowly, looking with large eyes and fixed gaze reproachfully at the woman. Then everything dissolved into barren sleep.

***

The next morning Kathrine Stumpf said to her daughter, "It was a funny dream."

"What dream?"

And she told her about it.

The girl went to the window and looked outside.

"Well, isn't it funny? Perhaps, who knows, it might mean something."

Marie pressed her face, glowing with shame, against the windowpane, and began to cry.

"Silly goose, it's a dream, it's not worth crying over."

"Oh, I'm not crying because of the dream. It's just so obvious — the ocean, the little bit of light around the poor, poor girl who'd like to call for help and can't talk, mustn't, just prays, in the air with bare arms."

She had said that haltingly, and her voice had often been dissolved into gasping by her impassioned crying.

"Well, that might be", Kathrine Stumpf pondered in helpless seriousness.

"Mother!", the girl cried, and turned her face to her, "Mother, would you help me if I, *I* was the girl?" Then she waited with morbidly rigid eyes and held her breath for an answer.

"Little Marie, I would and Wenzel too. — Don't make faces! Wenzel is a steady, industrious and clever man. Now leave off with the muttering against him, else he might leave us."

Then the girl's face turned pale and sad. She wanted to speak, but what she wanted to say she could not, and as she would have liked so much to say no, the thought of it made her blush. In embarrassment she stood motionless and forced a contemptuous sound through her nose, which should have been a laugh.

Then the sound of two dogs barking arose in the yard. Cutting sharp, yapping, baying sounds fought against harsh growls.

"I'll see what it is." She plunged outside hastily, breathing so cheerfully as if she had been about to do something evil, and was now freed from the compulsion to do it.

"Why, why can't she just put up with Wenzel!?" The mother was still shaking her head when Marie slipped back in timorously.

"And?", she asked the girl.

"Our Fipsl is lying in his kennel on the straw, and crying pitifully, and won't come out, and shouldn't, as a dog is standing in front of his kennel, black and shaggy, a muzzle like a calf, eyes green as poison, with crooked limbs, and it is prowling outside the kennel so our Fipsl is almost warped with fear. And when I came out and wanted to wave it away with a barrel stave, it bared its teeth at me straightaway like the devil."

"... like the devil?", a man's voice behind them repeated timidly, questioning.

Wenzel, having come through the back door from the field, had entered unnoticed, and heard Marie's words.

A deep weariness, a freezing seized him. Vacant and lost in angry intimations, he said it mechanically once more, "like the devil", and, with deep despondency, he rested his eyes on Marie.

"Yes," she flared up in the fervour of a long restrained hate, "yes, Fipsl is lying in *his* kennel, it belongs to him, to him! to him!! — And such a mongrel, such a sheep chaser you have never seen, such hunger in its belly and a stripe on its back, who will crush it ... who? ... who??"

Her breath failed her, she threw her arms in the air, and stared at her mother imploringly with large eyes.

The night's dream flared in her mother like lightning. So, just so had the girl looked at her that night, with the same helpless, pitiful eyes. In the end, it had not been a dream at all, not the rumbling, not the girl seeking help, in the ... end! ... and she drilled her blazing look into Wenzel.

But he was not paying attention to anything. He was standing motionless, and looking out the window.

"Rrrrm!"

The rough, deep growl was there again, and then, barking madly, the whining sounds started up.

It stabbed Wenzel in the chest.

He flared up, his eyes rolled ... "the devil!" — He stormed through the door without closing it. He was outside. The strange dog — it was, oh God! it was Meicke — sprang at him barking for joy — get! beat it with the stick! — The dog fled through the fence, over ditches and stone heaps as though thrown, its hair flying, spurting blood. Behind it was Wenzel, swearing, screaming, swinging his stick incessantly, short of breath, until exhausted, just like the previous time.

Mother and daughter were watching it all from the window.

"He's weakening ... but he's running ... don't you see? ... Now the dog is over the high wall. — Is he completely mad?? — ... Doesn't he see the ditch there? — Ha! ... he's stopping! ... Now? ... Is he over it? Little Marie, dearest little Marie! ... is he over it? My eyes are weak, what's happening?"

But the girl was grim about her mother's fears, "What does it have to do with us? If a sharp stone were lying in the ditch, wouldn't that be good?" And her face was indifferent and cold.

But the woman was trembling with the excitement, she wiped the windowpanes, wiped her eyes, ran into the yard, and looked out. But Wenzel did not appear at the top of the stone wall. So he must be lying in the ditch ... dead ... with broken bones ... The woman rushed out of the house, across the fields and groves and ditches.

Finally she was there. Where, where was he lying?

Here, flown with his chest in a desperate leap onto the edge of the deep, wide ditch, his hands digging spasmodically in the grass as though he could yet clamber into unconsciousness, his face to the side, deathly pale. A wide streak of blood stretched from his forehead across the grey-green grass.

The woman sprang into the ditch, ladled water with her trembling hand and trickled it onto the wound, once, twice, and more, with loving patience.

After a long time he began breathing ... his eyes were still shut, but he was smiling. "Ma ... Ma ... Ma", he slurred blissfully with half-dead lips.

Then he opened his eyes, and turned to her with a searching wistful look. When he saw the old woman, he shut them hastily, and a painful disappointment puckered his face.

"Love, dear love, have you broken anything?"

He shook his head and said nothing.

"Have you overworked your lungs?"

He shook his head, and a wild impatience clenched his face. His breathing stopped, none of his limbs twitched, it was as though he were dead. —

Suddenly he sprang up. Everything was revolving. "Dammit, that hurts!" But he clenched his teeth, and laughed, "So I'm standing! and the devil little Marie saw is gone!"

"And thank God! Let me feel your head please, poor thing, love ..."

"Hey!", he fended her off angrily.

They walked back to the yard together again.

Hermann Stehr

Wenzel's belief in the realisation of his plans had been shaken since Meicke had appeared at the farm again. It its place a secret fear, an unease came over him. Sometimes he sat for a long time in the sitting room and pondered with fixed eyes only to then spring up with a laugh, a scornful laugh like that which his hope had sounded in his soul when it had visited him that last time on the night with the trembling light.

But he did not laugh the fear away and his vanished hope did not return anymore.

It was still there, but he did not recognise it anymore. Its form had changed. It bore the form of little Marie and was striving against him. He reached out thousands of thoughts to her, thousands of thoughts, despondent, weak, but ardent and passionate. But they never entwined and danced, bound by chains in his soul. No, they rose like turbid flocks of migrating birds, looking with their longing eyes at him, and before he properly recognised them they had flown away into the grey of his sorrow.

"Gone since then, and now should that be all? Should I go now, because of a dog? — It's as if the laughter has bellowed my head empty, tearing the balls from my body so that I'm lying, empty and apart like the hut out back." — He spoke to himself thus when he was rolling around in the bed whose covers burned on him.

Then he lay, probably for hours, quite still, and he listened to the night. He had opened the window so every noise came through to him. Once it returned, the rough growling.

He had been waiting for it in order to put an end to it.

Now he heard it, he held his breath.

Quietly he pulled the cudgel out from where he had placed it under the bed, crept down the stairs, and plunged outside screaming an oath.

But Meicke must have heard the creaking of the bolt being pulled back, for Wenzel saw it like a shadow, and could only throw the cudgel after it, without hitting.

The nocturnal visits of the faithful dog were recurring more often now. But Wenzel never hit the dog, it avoided him so artfully. When he then returned angrily from such a nocturnal sortie, and lay in bed again, he would hear piteous howling in the distance. It was as though his misery were screaming at him, and shuddering he would drag the covers up over his ears so he could not hear it. But he perceived it with all his senses, and it was always Meicke who caused the despondency to come over his inner being.

— —

He was relaxing with a glass of beer on the hard bench of a tavern.

"You've a good dog", the landlady came up to him, "even if he isn't pretty."

With some effort, he hid his fright, and smiled distressfully, "Yes! yes! — haha!" and he looked out the window.

In fact the "bitch" was standing there outside in front of a horse, and looking wistfully up at it with its large, brown eyes. Then it walked around the wagon with slow happy steps.

A man strode past. Immediately the dog bared its teeth threateningly. After that it licked the dirt from the nag's ankle hairs full of tenderness.

"Have you got a gun?", Wenzel asked mutedly.

"For what?"

"That mutt must go, I've been irritated by some unpleasantness with it. Some shot will deal with the pain before it bites."

"No, and if I had one, certainly not for that."

Then he ran outside. But the dog had already disappeared. He headed off in a rush. But when he had arrived at the next tavern and, after a while, was looking out the window again, a black, sullied ball was lying under the tray of the wagon — Meicke! Broken down, emaciated to a skeleton, its tongue hanging out its mouth, and trembling.

He fled, but he could not cast off the dog!

When he looked up from his work in the forest, he noticed it in the distance creeping between the stems of the berries.

In the field, it suddenly emerged from a ditch lying a long way off, hesitated a while, laid its head to the side, and looked longingly at him for a moment. After that it disappeared into a ripe field of grain. The seedheads could be seen waving for a long time. The movement continued as far as the middle of the field. Then everything was motionless again.

The twilight glow was trembling alone again over the wide area just like his soul was quaking under the burden of a burning fear.

The girl under whose possession he suffered looked at him vacantly from the side. He felt that a cold hate lay in those eyes.

Ha! why had he been an ass in his ardency, in the trembling light, so that she had fled?

Could he not have waited until her mother led her into his arms?

What, eh, what had got into him anyway, because of that girl? Nothing! Without her, he'd become owner of the business! With a jab in the chest, he would have thrown her onto the street. But, that was madness! —

He had to make the girl more inclined towards him. How that could come about, he could not figure out. His diligence, his skillfulness, his gift for animated, momentous stories, nothing had worked so far. When she was a child, he had ignored her. Now she had reached eighteen years and hated him. Why? — She saw in him that which he was — the robber of domestic happiness, the destroyer of her reputation; the one who sullied the most sacred thing that a child carries in her heart, the image of her mother. By herself, she was too chaste to also guess at the sensual corruption of her mother. Only a great, boundless pity, that was her abhorrence. In the fever of her young-blooded, fervent sorrow she had sworn to rather die than allow Wenzel to touch her as well.

Thus the depths of the dreamlike world which blossomed in the bosom of her youth were closed to Wenzel.

He saw himself opposite a might which he was not equal to, since he did not understand it. Love is only obtained through love.

But this was hardly more than a bestial act to him.

Violence is no use. How else could he turn her?

Oh, this damned child!

And he worked, brooding, he slept, brooding, he sat in company, brooding — it was all in vain!

This impotence was corroding the fabric of his inner being like a poison. His diligence had slackened, he saw his honesty as a constraint, his care for the welfare of Kathrine Stumpf as a foolish stupidity.

Restlessly the dog orbited him. It did not just follow his steps, it ran after his thoughts, its barking tore up every plan, every decision holed up before its eyes, it hounded his willpower to complete exhaustion.

Finally, what he had feared for a long time eventuated.

The clear autumn stood in the sky, and it was oats harvest. On the stubble of the rye fields wafted the haze of the Indian summer, the September light lay across the expanse like a motionless cloud of gold dust.

Wenzel was standing in his short sleeves in an almost completely harvested field of oats whose long edge ran along the main road. Laying his arms on the crosstruss of a propped up rake, he watched a loaded harvest wagon rolling slowly to the barn. Kathrine Stumpf was striding next to it, and waving from time to time with the whip, behind her the girl was walking cautiously in her tracks.

He should, as it had been determined, have gleaned the few sheaves quickly, and then hurried after them in order to be of help with the unloading of the wagon.

He had worked the entire day lethargically. Now it seemed to him as though it was an entirely unfamiliar wagon that he saw there, an unfamiliar field in which he stood, as though they were unfamiliar people for whom he was working for free.

Such thoughts had already come to him often, but he had never let them win control over him. With bold fist, his courage constantly banished them, "Well, I once went into the church as a lad and came out again as a man."

But this exclamation had become more and more feeble. Today he said absolutely nothing and, with bitter face, he watched the wagon becoming indistinct in the dusty light of the distance.

In his inner being a yawning opened up, the dull inertness of the dispirited, the aimless lulling of a soul that knows it's lost.

Everything in his life had been reaped, like the field on which he stood! Others were taking the last fruits of his diligence into their barns, fruitless dead-rooted stubble remained for him. Ha, what did he get out of it other than that he was confronted with more respect since he wore a full coat? That was nothing other than a monotonous, pointless trudge.

"To the devil with it all!" He stamped down the rake so that its teeth struck dully in the earth, reached in his vest pocket to make certain that he still carried enough money on his person, shoved his cap back, slung his jacket over his shoulder, and strode whistling to the main road.

Good, today he wanted to see, for the first time in three years, whether he still had a taste for schnaps.

Down by the corner of the barn Kathrine Stumpf was standing and calling out to him. He laughed at the "witch", and flung himself steadfastly forward.

The woman was calling louder so that it sounded like the crowing of a hoarse rooster.

"Cock-a-doodle-doo," he scoffed, "your a little rooster, all noise, but the evening crows best of all, in Marie, yes, Marie ..."

An old man was hobbling towards him. He was hauling a cart behind him, and talking to himself, grumbling in the way loners and reprobates always do.

"Now, Grieger, old man, how goes it?"

The man addressed started in surprise. Then his gaze crept up timidly to the questioner. Then he recognised him.

"No, Jesus, Maria and Joseph, is it you? — Yes you, you can walk freely. But me ... still, it's like being a rubbish heap by the side of the road: everybody walks around me. — No bride, no gold, no wood, chills in my bones, and all rocks in my body. Nobody confides it quite so freely — how it goes. You probably never know how it goes for us poor devils. You've never eaten bacon like a mouse."

"Well yes, everything's well with me, and I've money ... haha ... look now, old man ..." He let his coins glitter in the palm of his hand before the man's greedy, dry eyes.

Now he was separated inwardly from his goal, he felt the need to speak boastfully about it to others.

"Right, as it is, I miss being angry, dancing, writhing, tossing my coat as the wind whistles. Grieger, such a steady man is a miserable man. You poor hussies don't know at all how free you are."

"Wenzel, look now, I don't understand that. I might just come to it if I'm full. Empty stomach, empty head." He shook his head in mute sorrow. Then his mood became grasping.

"Wenzel, do you want, look now, I am quite ... You well know, my place is freezing inside ... Give me one of those white pieces there", and he pointed timidly at a ten pfennig coin, "I haven't swallowed a thing today."

"Here, take it, and give my greetings to everyone."

"Thank you so much, thank you so much, that'll stretch, yes, yes!" After that he hobbled on, but he went faster, he was in a hurry.

The life into whose arms Wenzel stood on the point of throwing himself had appeared as a warning before him in its most exemplary image, an old drunkard. Alone he had no pride, no will, no sense of honour, no hope anymore, he was lost. He walked languorously under the trees by the main road.

The wind was rustling in them and the first withered leaves were falling on his shoulders.

"Yes, yes, autumn is returning", he thought, and headed unperturbed for the tavern.

Wenzel knew that his business at the farm was over. But he did not release the hold with which he had fastened the old woman to himself. It was not going of its own accord, that was definite. It would only yield to force. But then, if one should come, he would allude to what strong teeth he had. And the asses and load carrying, the work until late at night, it all stopped. He let the sun shine in his face. Then he climbed out of bed and breakfasted leisurely. He carried out the work for sport. He liked most of all to cruise around on the wagon, buying and selling what he found. He emptied the profit and something more into his pocket instead of the old woman's drawer. When Kathrine Stumpf was baffled over it, he shrugged his shoulders, and opined, "Well, the others have copied me, and it makes me nothing now; things are just weaker."

He was never at a loss for a reason to excuse his actions. When he came home late from the tavern, he had had to wait a long time on tardy debtors. When he was drunk, which also happened more often now, then the others had poured schnaps into his beer unnoticed, and he swore slurring at the rogues.

Soon he was lounging until midday, asking for better food since he deserved everything, and clothing himself like a dandy. Kathrine Stumpf watched full of anger the change in her partner's temper. But he was smart enough to keep her lust active, so she resigned herself, if also with misgivings, and sought her comfort in excuses for his actions.

She did not need them for her peace, but rather to appease her daughter, whose distaste for the dissolute business was expressed gruffer and more and more caustically.

"Oh look, little Marie, you must never lose your patience. Just think what I have saved over the years that Wenzel has been here, never in a long time would I have saved five hundred talers. The foremen simply look ragged in other places like mine. They sometimes have a dull patch. When it has passed over, then they are brisk and diligent again as before."

"Yes, yes, that dull patch, I won't argue with that, but there are also women who, it seems to me, are totally confused."

Laughing bitterly, she walked away, and tears were falling from her eyes.

Once Wenzel came home towards evening, a shot gun on his back and Meicke next to him, timidly nestling against his leg.

Mother and daughter both looked up at him, speechless, astounded. The old woman was first to find her voice, "Well, what should that be then?", and she pointed at the shot gun.

"Nothing," Wenzel burst out laughing, "I'm simply going hunting now."

"Yes! and what good is that then?", the repressed fury asked.

"None, do you want something to eat all the crops. Look how the barley stands there. And in spring the deer and horses eat half of it, and what they can't get at they trample. It is easiest for me to bang away at them."

Kathrine Stumpf looked at him, and since it flattered her vanity that her "employee" dared to go hunting like a "great landowner", she was quiet, and made do with murmuring something about a "crazy boy".

Marie had listened to the parley with her downcast smouldering eyes and held her breath. When she now heard her mother fall silent and, looking up, had to read satisfaction on her face, she lost all control over her hate, sprang up, grabbed a broom, and pounced on Meicke, which, baring its fangs, retired to the door, "Is that bitch back again too?"

"Put the broom away, the dog stays here, it's mine!"

"The dog! — staying here? — Out! — It stares like a devil!" And the furious girl bravely set on the dog, which did not find its courage in this unfamiliar place but stood in the corner of the door with its head against the wall and answered the unsparing blows swishing down with fearful growling.

In grim indecision, Wenzel watched for a while, but then he screamed, pale with rage, "Now that's enough! Such a faithful dog, and you belting it. Away, or I'll sic it on you."

But the girl was not listening.

"Meicke, alla ... sic 'er! ... sic 'er!!" Howling it turns around, quick as lightning, and burrows its fat head in the dress of its torturer so that it rips and splits open.

The women cry out in fright, and Wenzel whistles the dog off. It comes immediately, and places itself next to him. Its eyes are blazing green, its hair is standing up stiff as bristles on its back, ready for battle, it turns its head from the mother to the daughter and back again.

Both the intruders thus stood in open hostility opposite the owners of the house. —

Marie, pressed fearfully into the corner behind the table, looks persistently and chalk-white at the ground. Then she lifts her eyes in infinitely agonising humility, and looks at her mother for a long time, silent, bitter.

But she, under the man's spell, dares not say anything.

"Isn't this our house ... you ... you ... you?", gasps the poor girl with a failing voice which dies away in jerks under the swelling anguish.

The dog thus stays there, because, as Wenzel had explained to the all too believing old woman, he needs it for hunting. "For a hunter without a dog is like a fish without a tail."

It followed its master wherever he went, lay in front of his room at night, and jogged skillfully between the front wheels of the wagon on business trips.

Wenzel was never seen anymore without the dog whose understanding and faith he could not praise enough. But how he had come to accept it as his own — he told nobody. It had happened thus:

His intoxication had tossed him out of the tavern and onto the street. He had walked uncertainly, staggering toward his residence. His legs were suddenly humming stronger, ever stronger. They are becoming heavier, ever heavier. He is not raising them anymore, and plunges across the road, already asleep in the process. — Suddenly he feels himself being pulled. It is tugging on his arm, it shrilly howls in his ears. Now he feels a stab in his arm. Then he starts. Where is he? Whimpering a black dog draws its fangs out of the muscle of his upper arm. He wants to swear. At once there is a grumbling in the hard road, a thundering rattle is rolling nearer so that everything trembles. The fright tears his head up. Two lights are flickering up in front of him ... the devil, a wagon! ... the horses snorting! ... a wild sideways leap in mortal fear ... head over heels he plunges into a ditch, and is saved.

His intoxication seems to have been blown away. The dog, however, is licking the blood trickling onto his hand from the wound in his arm.

Then he pulls the ugly head up to his own, and presses a fervent kiss in the stinking shaggy hair. It is his ardent apology for everything he has done to it.

Never again does it leave his heel, for it has saved his life. —

After that the winter fell from the dead sky onto the dead earth.

It fell down like a berserker, a storm in each fist. And when it opened both fists and released the storms, then the world seemed lost.

Whipping, biting, snowy clouds pelted down, the forests thundered, the shingle rooves rattled, the defenceless bushes in the fields lay on their knees before it and begged for mercy. But the sympathetic stars closed their deep, beautiful eyes in fright when the thunderstorm broke forth.

The next morning when the sickly sun rose arduously and shivering, and saw the calamity that its dear earth had seen overnight, its countenance became even paler. But the people said, "Today isn't wanting any excess at all." — Yes, now came a sequence of those long, dreary twilights that are called winter days. When the light once broke fully over the laden mountains, over the wide plains, then people closed their eyes, as the freezing sunshine hurt them.

Breathing out, the people turn their backs on such days and flee through their narrow doors to the warm hearths in the half-light of their sitting rooms. There they talk to each other with gentle, drowsy voices about their hopes.

Kathrine Stumpf and Marie were also sitting at the table on such an evening, and you could see in their faces the joy of being alone.

The old woman was sitting by the wall and stripping feathers. Marie, opposite her, was knitting.

Several times, the girl let her knitted stocking drop, and looked at her mother the way one ponders a book whose content is indecipherable.

Her mother, however, lowered her eyes before her gaze, and plucked more assiduously at the feathers.

Then the girl's look became uncomfortable for her, and she said without looking up, "What are you always looking over at me for?"

"Oh, I was just thinking."

"About what?"

"How long will the winter last?"

"Now, a seasonal spring makes for a short winter."

"Isn't it, mother, that if the Lord were to miss making a winter, then there wouldn't be one."

"Well ... no ..."

"Do you like having a winter? You don't see anything, no sky, no sun, no green, no blue ... and you can't help it giving you that sinking feeling ... do you like having a winter?"

"No, little Marie ... no ..."

"Oh, I liked having one once. And when the snow came, it was as if my heart sang ... but now, I'd rather see no snow, and no slush, even if it only seemed like it's clear."

"Just as I came in last night I heard the slats cracking in the storm, and I got such a fright, such a fright, I couldn't see at all ... and I always just pondered, well, what if the wind takes you and drives you far, far away so the mountains can't see you anymore. I thought about it, I don't know, it was like that all day with me ... and it never left me, that 'far away over the mountains'." —

"Yes, you'd like to go, and without me?"

"No, mother, never without you. But I pity you so, oh mummikins, dearest mummikins", and she threw herself crying around her mother's neck. But her mother trembled under the embrace as though under an incrimination.

"Go, go! you're pushing the feathers all over the place. — — — — I don't know what comes over you?!", and, trembling, she pushed her daughter away.

Saddened, the girl went back to her place.

She looked rigidly at her knitting. The tears were running silently over her cheeks, and she furtively wiped them away with hasty fingers.

The fire sobbed in the hearth. Then it was as if something were whining.

"The man in the fire is singing! — What does that mean, mother, good or bad luck?"

"I don't know."

"It must be a poor soul who couldn't help himself and acted so mean that the Lord burnt him to cinders."

"Stop it, girl, it'll wake him proper."

Thus the child, for she was a child despite her eighteen years, stirred the maternal soul restlessly with dreamlike words so that the woman despised herself in her heart.

As though Marie had read her innermost thoughts, she began,

"Where does he stay so long?"

"Now, he will be out hunting."

"Don't they ever shoot somebody by mistake?"

"Oh now ... but that is bad luck."

"Bad luck? ... Perhaps the man in the fire was singing so terribly because of that."

If it would be, if she would not see him anymore, swearing in anguished lust, breathing furiously, then, oh, then everything would be right once more! —

Her mother was thinking that — no, it came over her like a weeping, fervent prayer so that she fell silent, and looked at her daughter with wistful eyes.

"Listen, Fipsl is barking. Now he's coming!"

"How late is it?"

"Half past eleven."

"Half past eleven", her mother repeated to herself grimly.

The piping bark of the little guard outside set off the familiar, deep growling.

Between the barks, shuffling, staggering steps were heard. Groping, he grasped at the wall under the window. Now he was holding onto the door. Then he was shoving and working his way around it.

Kathrine Stumpf sprang up to open it.

"Mother!" —

The girl said the one word, only the one, but with such abhorrence, so gravely, that the woman awoke from the hypnosis of her lust, and willingly returned to her place. She sat there motionless, and not daring to raise her eyes anymore.

Meanwhile the door flew open.

Wenzel swore, and laughed confusedly.

He stopped at the entrance to the sitting room.

"Here, Meicke, come in. I'm the boss here. If you're disturbed, then I'll shove the house over, ha, ha, dam..."

Then it was completely silent for a while. He was obviously considering whether or not to go into the sitting room, and decided after some pondering in favour of the latter.

"What says the dog, Meicke, what ... what ... what!! ... says ... the do...g?"

The dog barked sharply.

"Hello, old boy! That wasn't needed at all, no, I'm *not* inclined at all, I'm the boss, me and you, as we have balls, haha!"

Then he rumbled up the stairs.

Kathrine Stumpf was trembling, and it was as if her soul were crumbling before her daughter's eyes, which rested wide and clear on her.

But her mouth formed no words, as she was so deeply, so deeply ashamed.

After that they reached out their hands to each other in order to say, "Good night."

Neither spoke a word.

The press of her fingers was limp, cold, and past hope.

In that way Kathrine Stumpf lay herself down to sleep, and in that way she rose — in hopelessness.

After a few days, it became horror. Her senses looked at her relationship with Wenzel as though with averted eyes.

She was afraid to agitate it by direct aim. For a fear sat threateningly in the depths of her wrecked soul.

And when it sat upright in the woman, tormented by her burden, and in just hatred of the, yes now, the rogue tumbling over her threshold, then all her past would awake, all her sins which lay under the mildew of ever fresh delinquencies, and she felt that she had to expose herself with her entire past existence to a new spirit that had come into her.

She had no strength for it, hence she was frightened.

The new spirit had come into her gradually.

That night when she had imbibed the ardency from the trembling, blue light, that night its germ had been born. Slowly, imperceptibly it had grown. Sometimes it seemed to have died or emigrated. Then it was again sucking beady-eyed on the fiery breasts of her lust. Yet, often in the middle of the stammering of her sins, it was there again. But she was becoming discerning. Her overflowing body was sinking back. The slurring of her passion merged into a raw scream so that the man fled in fright from her room, and left her alone with her anguished crying.

When her loathing had freed her heart, the new spirit settled permanently and took up residence in her. Then, when the wild urge wanted to climb out of the glimmering, it rose up and gently travelled through her with a clean swing. And — — she let her eyelids fall over her blazing eyes and left her hand on her beating heart until she was breathing regularly again under the reins of unobscured reflection.

After every victorious overcoming of such an attack, a stronger and stronger sense of well-being came over her, a stronger calm. A peaceful light resided in the soul's wounds that made her smile blissfully.

"Mother, when you laugh like that, you aren't like a woman at all", her daughter would then say to her.

"How do you mean then?", she asked happily.

"Well, now, where else would I see it, like — a — child who finds the first flower in its life, like that."

"Well then", and she turned quickly away, and went back to working with trembling hands, because she had to think about having lost something which must have been infinitely beautiful and sweet.

Then she could not get away from it for days, and it laid a retrospective longing in her, a heavy dreaming full of wistfulness. She had forfeited something glorious before she had possessed it. She could not detect what it was. Only a strong, deep, lasting aversion to Wenzel arose in a mysterious way from her brooding.

Not just from her brooding alone, but also from the brusque way that Marie confronted the intruder, from her hard words, her scornful looks. Yes, and bit by bit, the more often she looked at her daughter, especially when her big eyes laughed freely in a peaceful, happy shimmer, it became as though it was begining to dawn in her that every lost soul must have possessed such looks.

It was making her sad, and she avoided every contact with Wenzel, for she recognised that her relationship to him was the last link in the chain with which she had strangled every beautiful thing in her life's distant past.

Her being had thus been reborn into sorrow and self-torment, under a trepidation and under enormous, secret longings, from a life which had tumbled in dull straw, wandered between ditches and nooks, and finally fled hither with the savings of vice in order to enjoy in comfort the dregs from the cup of lust.

Hence, her new spirit was a torment, a heavy, black cloud over her soul.

But outside, far away where the dimly lit contours of the island of her youth were dawning, it stood and waved, silent, beautiful, infinitely sweet — an angel, a sun, a spring, did she know? — And she stretched her arms out to it across the shadows of her life's morass.

Wenzel did not know what was happening in the old woman. He just saw her altered temper.

As though in flight, she was now constantly shoving past him. During their meal times together, she sat mutely there, seldom even exchanging a word with her daughter.

His visits to her bedroom were long since over, and her eyes were always so quiet, cold and certain, her mouth so serious and silent that to him the atmosphere was constantly dying away in ambiguous laughs, although his shrewdness had advised him a hundred times already, "to pour oil in the lamp".

Slowly but surely he was forced from his commanding position into that of a worker. A blind eye was turned to his debaucheries, his neglect of the work, his shooting. They did not want, his sharp-eyed distrust told him, to disturb his feeling of security, all the more to arrange unfettered and thoroughly all preparations for the final divorce. He saw everything, grasping precisely that the earlier unrelenting friction between mother and daughter had ceased completely. The business measures were being discussed between the two of them. The carrying-out of those measures was conveyed to him curtly and explicitly.

On the 2nd of January, the "rump day", i.e. the moving day for servants, he was requested by Kathrine Stumpf to wait after breakfast for something. She sent Marie outside.

He wanted to sit close by her on the bench.

"Go and sit yourself down on the bench. I would have to stand up again straightaway."

"As you wish!", he resigned himself with seething laughter.

"On New Year's it became four years that you've been with me", she continued without paying any attention to his laugh.

She spoke softly, shaking, with a trembling resolve.

"You have gotten up to now nothing but clothing and food. I never wanted that. For you are a ... an able, clever and, and a good man. You were a pillar to me ..."

"... were ...", he repeated, and whistled gently over his drooping lower lip.

"Were", she nodded firmly. "Beggars reward themselves with gifts, I don't. If you want to stay here on a wage then that's okay, if not, I'm sorry. You must simply move out by 1st of April."

He had not expected that. He supported his head on his left hand, shoved himself back a bit from the table, and drew out his toneless "you, you, that" in helpless fury.

Then he sprang up fiercely.

"Meicke!"

The dog placed itself next to him.

He walked up to her, threateningly, and his lower lip shuddered.

"Tell me, Kathrine ..."

"Stumpf", she interrupted him.

"Never mind! — What is this?"

"A dog", she forced a laugh.

"No, it's a bitch! — Why is that then?"

She shrugged her shoulders fearfully, and looked to the door.

"No you won't, haha, you're staying here." Hastily he bolted the door, and returned.

"Why? – shall I go over it? – Because I can trust it, spit on it, cast it out, do what I want, and it won't do anything, no. Because of that, it's a bitch", and he had bent down in front of her, and had shaken his pale face quite close to hers. Then he heaved himself upright, and rushed to the middle of the room where he paused with a jerk, laughed in a corner and, after a few thoughts, returned again.

"What does the dog say to you?"

It was as though the man's fury had been transferred to the dog. It sprang up, hurtled around with its hindlegs pawing at the floorboards, and gave that judderingly sharp noise that resembled the whistling of a bullet.

Wenzel nodded contentedly.

"And what is that?", he asked coldly and tonelessly.

The woman did not dare to stir anymore.

"Right, you never thought about that, no, no. You see, I will be watching — when the bitch attacks, and tears you apart!"

She had understood him only too well, and sat there in a daze.

"And now you come once more and free me — do you want a wage? — That is as if you said, Meicke, bite everything!!" —

The dog became threatening, climbed up on its hindlegs, and waited with blazing eyes for a second shout to be able to fall on the crumpled woman.

But Wenzel calmed it with strokes, and then left the room with strong strides, and without once looking back.

I n vain! She never made it across the expanse of rubble to the beckoning horizon.

No way out!

She went about as though under the dullness of a blow.

Her thoughts were screaming.

She moved about restlessly, full of animation, and yet she did not tackle anything anymore.

Before every bit of work, she had the feeling that she must do something beforehand.

Giving up hope, she strove for blessing.

She found it alone, after she had waited for weeks.

It was behind the barn, where a small meadow lay.

The midday sun seemed hot, and the snow was glistening.

In front of her stood a bin full of ashes. She had pushed the shovel in, and paused, for it occurred to her again that she must do something first. And because she could not work it out again, she looked emptily and bleary-eyed into the winter.

The road led over there, lonely, wintry bleak.

Only a boy was walking along it.

He was probably kept in at school, and was running so that the school things in his wooden satchel could be heard clattering.

The forest was not stirring. It was noiselessly calm. A distant bell heaved into tolling, pure, sweet, lovely, like a childish request, a soft, fawning exhortation.

And other bells, quite distant with obscured tones, quite near with vibrating blows, repeating what that first one had sung.

The little boy on the road, as he heard the air speaking with the iron tongues of the bells, stopped running, took off his cap, hid his little hands under it and prayed.

The woman next to the bin also sank to her knees, for the spirit of her youth had finally found its way to her and blessed her soul.

She had waited a long time for what had finally arrived.

She was able to pray again.

After that, she watched dreamily for a while, stood up straight, and threw the ashes over the glistening snow in powerful swings so that the spring flowers would want to sprout out of the ice.

The day passed in happy silence for her. She was glad when Marie sought her bed straight after supper, because she did not feel quite well. For the woman now had a longing for her own company, and wanted to be alone. But Wenzel forced her into all kinds of conversation in order to detain her still longer. At the same time, he was often looking at her quite fixedly.

She was just wanting to stand up in order to scurry past him to her bedroom when he grasped her wrist, and roughly restrained her.

"Wait a moment, I have something to tell you."

Then he pondered for a while, looking at the floor, shook his lowered head a few times, and murmured something indecipherable.

"Say it and go", the woman urged.

"It's no use to you, none — none — at all", the words finally came over his lips, broad, slow, and fiercely bitter.

Then he waited a while without raising his eyes.

But the woman did not ask and, from deep thought, he continued speaking, more to himself, spiritlessly.

"That about costs — for rent — by the bell ... for I married you. Where you go, I go ... where you stand, I'll be ... no step without me ... the woman kneels when she prays for the man to stay ... it's the same, for the one inside raising her hands up … it's the same and no use, no use at all — none."

His agonising breath whistled into a long silence.

"Meicke, come!"

His voice's deep seriousness weighed on the dog so much that it crept to him on its belly.

"Kathrine, do you feel vengeance, the pain, the chaffing." The woman reluctantly did.

"See, everything's been destroyed, crumbled, scarred … oh, how it looked!"

And becoming wilder, "And my hands grasped it, strangled it, bent it to breaking … I wanted to make an end to the misery, to the men, to the schnaps — — — I prayed, I prayed to him above, just like you — — —." Then he pointed at the dog, "It fled into the night, it barked and disappeared — — — it was so easy for me then, so easy! — For it's no dog, it's the devil, all that the man has to curse for it to turn out alright for him is the dog, my misfortune … ha! — But you see, it's all no use, clapping the hands over your head, none — at all — none! — it stands there again and looks at me — and everything that you loved in me is gone from me again like castles in the air … everything, everything. — And it looked for a moment, a … but you are like a sister-in-law … Go and pray, it's no use, none, none …", and while he was repeating the word, he released her, and staggered outside without lifting his head.

It seemed to the woman as though he had shrunk.

This incident strangled her hopes to a senselessness. She sat in the church ... she knelt before the crucifix in the forest, before the cross in the fields — — — she spoke through the grill of the confessional with pale, trembling lips. — —

The bells tolled. The forest rustled austerely. The clouds in the sky bowed to her graciously. The Father's friendly voice promised her forgiveness ... and ... it was yet in vain.

She did not cart it off from before her ears, nor bring it out from her soul, that despairing, hollow *no use, none, none.*

In vain. — — —

Meanwhile it was becoming spring outside. The woman did not see it until the starlings were singing in the trees, and she walked through the youthful sunshine with her aged sorrow. —

But Marie was exulting in the light.

For a different spring had awoken in her.

Her eyes, otherwise so empty, were shining friskily. But when she cautiously crept back to the sitting room from the garden's shadows in the deep twilight of the evening, then they smouldered fierily, and her lips were moist and swollen red from the secret potion of first love.

But her mother was not aware of anything.

Just once did the shimmer in her daughter's eyes attract her attention. She paused, and dreamt in the pure light, and she thought wistfully of the beauty she had lost before she had possessed it.

For emaciated by the delights of the flesh, exhausted by a lusting will, she had lost the strength for a clean separation, and was now wandering on the borders of the good, a sleepwalker of purity.

One pair of eyes, however, saw clearly, because they observed everything through the burning glass of jealousy.

Nothing escaped them. They even noticed the shadow of a man walking out of the garden into the moonlit field each evening, and then shut firmly, because the seething blood was shooting painfully into them.

Only one pair of eyes saw clearly, and Wenzel cursed them, because they were his own, and he cursed everything they saw.

But he could not change it. And if he had torn them out of their sockets, from under his labouring brow, those glowing coals, the spell would not have been destroyed which dreamed every evening in sweet secrecy, there in the transparent shadows of the trees.

He walked around gently, timidly. His soles shuffled across the ground. He was afraid of treading firmly. Hate had filled his breast with decided impulses of which every one was like a mine with dry tinder.

Only a spark needed to fall in it, into the heavily burrowed interior, and the dynamite would discharge itself in fierce action. But he was fearful of the sparks, for he knew that it would then be over with everything, with everything, even with his life.

That's why he walked so gently, so cautiously, so as not to wake his wild ego to sudden decisive leap.

Gritting, he held back Meicke who lurked faithfully next to him, trotted nervously and whined with impatience when the two young people were softly stirring each other, tipsy with happiness.

Each evening, Wenzel stole after the girl who was sneaking out, and he crouched behind the woodpile next to the barn.

Each evening, he vowed to chase them both away.

But then the jealousy always lay like a feverish daze over him, so his eyes just burned trembling under the tightly pressed eyelids, and his lips murmured incoherent words of vindictiveness.

On a Sunday in May, a spark ignited the hidden embers of his inner being.

Dinner had been cleared away. The washed dishes stood on the drying rack again. Wenzel had gone straight after the clearing away to his room, to sleep, as he had said with a sharp look at Marie. Mother and daughter were sitting together on the bench, and doing what is usual in May, they were looking outside.

The window stood open. Sunshine, the good cheer of finches, and the scent of blossoms poured in.

Kathrine Stumpf passed her hand over her brow to wipe something away from her thoughts. But she still remained pale and distressed. The girl, however, was fervently breathing in the bliss of the world outside.

"Go, girl, I want to rest a little. Go into the garden and sing, I'd like so much to hear a young girl singing." Marie skipped outside and a simple school song soon rang out into the tree nursery's dreamily rustling roof of blossoms. But not for long, as her vitality was breaking down the barriers of the song. The girl's voice was indulging itself, the song's words and its artfully wandering rhythm rose to an exultation in which was mixed yearning jubilation. The song had turned into a call of yearning love.

In the sitting room, her mother supported her head in her hands and listened for a while. When the flooding and tactless indulgence began, she was upset, "What is that about? That'll make no sense to anyone." — Then she lay down on the hard bench, her hands under her head, and began a humming sleep.

Suddenly it seemed to her as though she had been stabbed in the heart. Her breath faltered in fear, and she sat up with a jerk. The sun had already strolled futher towards the mountains and was sending golden rays through the window to the right of the table and across the sand strewn floorboards. For a while, she watched, astonished and confused by the trembling light. Then it made sense to her that she had become confused over such an everyday occurrence. Meanwhile, what had happened that had raised her with a jolt from her sleep? She found herself alone in the room, what was it ... then the drowsy fluctuations of her thoughts were ripped apart by Meicke's wild barking. She is fully lucid at once, stands up, and goes to the window. The dog runs from the garden as though it has been driven away by someone, pauses, bristles the hair on its back, barks once more, and then springs in large bounds through the front door, and up the stairs with its claws striking loudly.

Down below she sees her daughter standing close next to a man. The girl has laid an arm on his shoulder, and both are looking in the direction the dog has taken.

Their faces are glowing in the chaste light of May, so that they look like two flowers in bloom. Now double-voiced, exuberant laughter rings out. Then they lean against each other and kiss, kiss without breaking off, as though they are completely alone in this world, as though no one were watching.

Above her, the upstairs window is shoved open with a rattle. Alone, she is not listening anymore, for in her heart the depths of her soul, the golden and the pure of her yearning, are becoming vast and growing and stretching over her wrecked past, over the shadows so that all her peace is in the light. She sees the beautiful life that she had forfeited before she possessed it — the pure love, the epiphany, her God — and she folds her hands, and blesses her flesh and her soul, resurrected to a new being in the life of her daughter.

Oh, that she could escape from that other, that gleaming curse which floats on every breeze, walks on every street, lurks in every room, and throws her child-eyed soul into chains! — —

If she could escape from it, her child! Above all else, she wanted to buy that, the dearest that she now had, with her life.

And as she pondered so, the stairs creaked gently with creeping steps.

Wenzel!

Now, right now! and he, he? — Where is he going? And she knows, in her embarrassment, nothing better to do than to kneel on the floor. But above her is the open window.

The steps shuffle across to the door ... outside ... to the wall ... now, in front of it ... no, now further on to the right, they stop ... she hears everything completely, completely clear, even the grains of sand under his soles crunch so clearly in her hearing ... like ... the hammer of a gun which — — — is — — — drawn — — noiselessly, she springs up in a stony fear. There!! — — —

If she stretches out her arm, she can grasp the barrel of the gun which is being raised trembling.

Now he is standing ready to shoot, stiff, as though nailed to the spot.

Everything is clear to her.

With a sudden grasp, she tears the gun's muzzle away, towards her breast.

The shot cracks and, twitching noiselessly, she sinks down.

Steps tumble away. Steps come flying. The door is torn open, and Marie throws herself wailing on the woman lying there.

"Oh, mummikins, dearest mummikins, stay with me — — look — — look oh, — I could have told you — — now, now it comes — oh ..."

The woman opens her eyes, fixed and questioning, in fearful maternal worry.

Marie understands the look, "He is gone, into the bushes with his gun and the dog, the accursed!"

Outside a shot thundered in the forest, and the echo rolls like clods falling into a finished grave.

"Freed!", the girl murmurs, and a shiver is convulsing her.

Her mother closes her eyes once more, and nods her head.

"Look, mother, and this is my dearest, my man, your son, get well, mother! ..."

The man who was standing there stiffly turned red after her confession. The tears were running copiously over his cheeks, his hard hands were grasping each other spasmodically, and nothing passed over his lips but a stifling, "Mother!"

She was watching them so blissfully, so encompassing of the two, and then she smiles once more the smile that makes her look so young.

With that she dies.

***

But Meicke, the devil, ran away from his master's grave, and after he had wandered about for a long time, he attached himself to the heels of another. —

The Inspector

Inspector Vogt was sitting there now like a child who wants to be better. His old mother was standing behind him, stroking his cheeks and bending down from time to time to press a kiss on his forehead with her toothless mouth.

"Now, Willy dearest, you will make it so that your old mother can laugh once more before she dies."

Willy stroked his blonde whiskers thoughtfully and nodded his head lifelessly as though it was connected to him by a completely foreign mechanism, by a chain of thoughts which had seized his soul, enslaved his soul without his desiring. His eye was dilated, and in its blue, back where the character's facial expression originated, it was arrayed softly, like a mist that has taken the leaves from the trees and buried the roses. At the same time, he was tapping with the heel of his right riding boot. It sounded to him as though he was nailing a coffin. He pressed his teeth together, his beard bristled on his cheeks, and, without his wanting, the old life, full of his soul's fury, whispered in his ear, "Dying — — snoring — droning, droning ..."

A chill shook the body of the old woman.

"My child," she consoled him with a pleading voice, "my child, believe me, you don't live through what you enjoy, but through what you do without."

He would have liked to have cried out, I don't want to deny myself though; I just don't want to believe anything, I want to experience everything — all that foolishness with which life exhilarates, whose fate it is to always have to remain at the beginning.

But as he turned around and looked up into his mother's eyes, from which a tear was detaching itself, he felt ashamed. And the power which lay in his mother's eyes took power over him, sparing and deep like words from the Bible. His soldierly will leapt to its feet, the riding whip fell to the floor.

"Now, so we want thus to play for a heart instead of money, and instead of riding up we want to ride in ..."

"Willy!", his mother interrupted him painfully. Vogt abruptly broke off his crunching laugh and sprang up.

"Here, mother, your hand. Sit down — over to the right!"

He locked the old woman in his arms.

The beatitude of her heart skipped into his soul and filled its clefts with pure feeling. Outside, the wizened leaves were falling from the elms in front of the window. They were groping their way cautiously downwards through the mist as though they were frightened of plunging and hurting themselves.

Willy watched.

He still had his right arm slung around the slender body of his mother.

Why did it appear only proper to him, this sedate descent of the leaves?

Yes, and how childish it was, that which he then asked as though caught in a dream, "Death, though, has no germ?"

The old woman knew nothing of the wavering of his deepest soul. She just caressed his cheek and whispered happily, "My Willy, my dear, good boy!"

Then she went home and the inspector stood at the gate. He watched the carriage until the mist broke up behind it.

Then it still hummed weakly to him like a writhing storm in the distance. He listened ardently as the music died away into a far off, beautiful distance which he would never see again.

"Now then never, never again ...", he said toughly, full of burdensome remorse. Then, with bowed head, he returned with slow steps.

***

All is well.

Willy was sitting as owner on his family's old estate, "Moschen".

The blonde Mika Exts, the daughter of the General-Director of the princely Orrinisch estates from neighbouring Nesselnitz, had become his wife.

Old Mrs Vogt had thus not prayed in vain for her son.

Old Exts had gifted his daughter the estate as part of the dowry. Thus the mother was granted presumably what she had begged God for all these years — that she might be permitted to die under her own roof.

She strode restlessly through the rooms in which she had enjoyed the short happiness of her marriage full of disappointments. And as she walked back and forth, the old images of her life broke through the young splendour from the joints of the walls where they had slumbered indestructibly and wandered after her feet, talked without break from the corners, and grew pale as dreams before her. She sat herself in a corner and tolerated with a sort of satisfaction that the memory wandered past her eyes on bridges in the air.

When she had at the time been driven after barely two years of marriage over the threshold of this house, she had lifted her Willy up and shown him the crowns of the trees which stood all around the lordly seat, "My baby, see, that is your father's house; now it will be foreign to us, poor child!" Then she had gone away without turning around and had taken refuge at the estate of her brother.

Her flight had apparently not touched her husband at all; he abandoned himself all the more exclusively to the ways of his mad blood and remained the "wild Hussar" right through to his death. Under the appplication of the refinements of a playboy, the modest wealth of his family had soon disappeared. Ruin arrived via neglected pastures, drove the cattle from the stalls, turned the equipment into junk and then strode across the desolate farmyard to knock at the creaking door of the homestead. During an evening hour, this rattling became painful for the "mad Hussar". He tore his own nag from the cold stall and rode away swearing.

He trotted home late at night, drunk. At the edge of his estate, where a bridge with high parapet led over the small stream, the ruin waited in ambush for his return, and when the first hoof beat thundered on the boards, it slipped from its hiding place and grew in garish plainness before the nag's head. The drunk recognised it more deeply than usual and, with a cry of fright, he pulled the nag back so that it stumbled backwards over itself. The unlucky man was found the next morning lying in the way with broken neck.

For them, his wife and son, nothing was left, for every nail was mortgaged. They would have had to suffer hardship if her own wealth had not been saved by the attentiveness of her brother. Thus she had watched, worried and prayed over the happiness of her Willy in the isolation of her brother's farm, humbled by her fate. But the mad blood, the inheritance of his father, obtained more and more power over him and began to tear his life from one whirlpool to the next.

For a long time she was afraid as a mother, then as a woman of being stranded on the same cliffs.

But Willy had finally accepted her wish and now all the whirl in the old waters of her life seemed to have smoothed out and all the disconsolate pictures of her memory assumed soft, happy colours.

Just then she wanted to begin again the wandering through the old-fashioned large rooms when in the next room the door was torn open, hasty steps stormed in and then suddenly stopped.

The pale face of the old lady brightened abruptly with a light redness.

"Willy, boy, is it you?", she called and hurried to him.

"Yes, certainly, mother, it's me!", he answered, approaching her. They met on the threshold. In happy awe, the son embraced his mother and kissed her.

"So you are now there for ever then?" Mrs Vogt asked, beaming.

"Yes, it is all happily overcome."

"But, where is Mika?"

"You can imagine, over there. After all the long travelling about the world, she feels like a daughter returning home. To be expected. What?

— Now you see and I trotted over quickly. This evening we finally arrive. But I wanted to see you once more, you know, just as a son. — For that is also overcome now — as I see."

With that he let his eyes wander over all the splendour and laughed hard, no, hostilely.

"Are you perhaps not happy with the way I've arranged it? Come and see first before you judge!", the old mother answered this laugh which shocked her and which she thought best to answer with a gentle ribbing.

"No, no, come and see", she took the words up more urgently again when he remained standing indifferently.

"Let it be, mama, I know you have good taste. I did not mean it that way either," he answered and could not prevent a certain irritation shimmering through his heartiness.

"But, little Willy, why don't you want to see everything then?", his mother asked.

"Ah, I'd rather we walked in the garden."

And he let the embracing arm fall from her body and they turned to the door out, Willy striding ahead, Mrs Vogt following with eyes lowered.

But at the door, the son let his hand drop from the handle again and turned around.

He looked in her face and recognised that his mother felt the same as him.

So he simply said, "It is of no importance at all."

And at her dismay, he repeated it with soft yet firm voice, "Totally, entirely of no importance."

"Then you are not happy ...", his mother stuttered.

Willy smiled in a forced way, though amiably.

"That too, mother, is also all the same", he said.

"I don't understand you, boy", she answered, apprehensively.

"Oh, my God, don't you rejoice over everything? — Yes? — Well, that is okay; see, that is indeed the main thing. Now we'll walk a little in the garden if you like."

The mother said nothing, but rather walked sadly next to him.

Even down in the garden, as she sat on a bench and Willy stood before her, leaning lightly against a tree, the mother felt more and more distinctly that she had become a thief for her son through the happiness to which she had helped him. This idea stood like a hot, torturous air about her soul, like a wavering veil to which she must always look while Willy told her of his honeymoon trip with Mika. He wove in his high-spirited jokes here and there, as always; but his mother just curled her fine, withered lips in response. Finally her fear cut through his muddled narration, "So are you really not happy, Willy?", she asked with effort.

Then he took the dear, creased face in his hands, bent it up to himself and pressed a kiss on her forehead.

"Mother," he then said, "the loneliness does not do you well; see, why do you focus in on one point which can't be changed anymore? We ruin everything, happiness and unhappiness, with thinking."

He had again returned to his tree as he said that; but his mother only looked with pale face silently before herself.

"Mother! – What do we want from us? — Nothing!"

She nodded slowly at the ground.

"Now, we don't recognise the effects of changes on ourselves either. We hope for the best. Am I not healthy and strong? And Mika is certainly a very loving, oddly clever being. How should that turn out to my misfortune?"

The hot, torturous air about the old soul was becoming more and more painful though as a result of this talk. —

Willy prepared then to return home. When the stable lad who had led the horse to him had gone and the son made ready to climb into the saddle, his old mother grasped his arm passionately and pressed it against her face, "Willy, but I only really wanted you to be happy, I did not act with any trace of self-interest."

Then she looked pleadingly and humbly up to him.

He, however, sprang as if shocked into the saddle.

"Now it is really high time though that I rode off and fetched Mika. — You, you!", he threatened her with his finger.

She wanted to say something more; but he cut her talk off, "It's no use, in at most three hours we will meet, then you shall see how we can bicker!"

With that he rode away from there. From the depth of the alley, he waved once more to the old lady standing by the lower gate who watched after him. Then horse and rider were still just a little point. Slowly she turned around and strode to the house. On the steps she reminded herself that she would now have to look again at all the new splendour. Full of fear, she climbed up through the back door to her simple rooms.

***

It was at the time of day when the impatient night looks with eager stars to the evening which tears itself from the waning once more again to wavering, but all the sharper images, wastes away, flickers once more with ever madder clarity, but finally sinks to the foot of the trees, deathly tired. At this time, as the souls of day and night flow into each other, like the souls of the dying and the long since passed away flow in death, Mika and Willy travelled from Nesselnitz to their remote estate. They had left so late that they had given up on the thought of finding Willy's mother still awake, and as a result they travelled quite slowly on the bumpy way through the wonders of early spring.

The hedges were dreaming their first little leaves. Behind the clods of the field, the broken-off blissful sighs of the first larks' songs were leaping up. Across the meadows, the transparent mist was drawing like dreams of youth. Far off lay the mountain forests which seemed to be plunging from the shimmering heaven to the earth like a giant cataract.

Mika was lying in the corner of the carriage and looking with sparkling eyes up at the blue abyss over her which people call the heavens.

Willy's eyes were bound by something invisible which he looked at with painfully distorted mouth while his hands turned his pocketknife back and forth nervously and made the blade click back from time to time.

Finally he tore himself away with a gesture the way you throw down a forced work which you cannot get right, and he asked with utter ease, "Mika, what are you thinking when you're looking up at the starry heaven?"

"My God, it looks like a young heart."

"Well, can be, so of what age?"

"Well the age at which the heart still rules over the head."

"There you are thinking of the blue, that deep without objects."

"For that reason, now certainly, why not then, I just call it unbounded enthusiasm ... being drunk on beauty ... rush of belief ... the age when the thoughts are nothing, like fragile, puny little ships on the seas of our soul, you see, small and illuminated like those tiny little points in this boundless, shimmering desolation up there above us."

"A foolishness ...", Willy answered in a dully thoughtful way.

"Certainly, my dear old fellow, even *the* foolishness; but *the* foolishness which first makes our life rewarding."

"I know, I know quite well," Willy answered earnestly, "and yet up there above us the beauty falls again and again into ruins and it is good to also think of that."

"I have thought of that too", Mika replied, "the comparison came to be for just that reason; but think how large a person's heart must be if not only the beauty of this earth, but also a world no man has yet seen finds a place in it."

"Mika, tell me please, why do you not have any red ribbons on your dress ... um ... haha!"

But when Willy saw that his young wife drew back into her corner at this mockery, and withdrew her hand which he had reached for, he began with ironic pathos, "In the hidden fabric of eternal laws of this contradictory material ..."

Then he pulled the pouting woman to himself and kissed her face, full of hot passion.

When both were again sitting "well-behaved", Mika began against her promise, "See, I wanted to say, such a starry world falls without trace. Can such a world of the heart then also perish — so that no breath, no shadow recalls it! as you said."

The unsuspecting woman knew nothing of the secret fears in the soul of her husband as she spoke so. His face gradually assumed an expression of shock, for the certainty of his fate came over him dully and hotly.

"Willy, you must speak", Mika admonished impatiently.

"Now, if you absolutely desire it — yes", he answered his fear and her question from the depths of his chest.

"Gone, completely gone?"

"Yes ..."

"So that no sound forces through its being anymore, like the waves of a silenced ringing."

"Yes ..."

"Also, does such a man have a hole in his breast into which the orphaned thoughts can throw themselves in order to wail?"

"Mika, my wife, such a man must not have anything anymore ... nothing ... nothing more ... nothing at all."

Then he clenched his teeth as though in pain.

"But, Willy dearest, what's the matter with you then?", she cried in shock.

"Nothing at all", he forced a smile.

On the right side of the road, a simple stone cross with gilded saviour on it appeared.

"Look", he said, and diverted his wife, "here is where my father had his accident."

And he thought to himself, the dead return though.

The carriage travelled past the cross slowly.

Willy and Mika had clasped each other's hands.

Then they were jolted forward sharply, for the horses leapt shying to the side as their hooves thundered on the boards of the bridge with the high parapet. Then they shotahead in a long trot, snorting.

The trees were dancing above them like laughing maidens. The wind was whistling bright chords in the tree tops. The mating call of the partridge was wandering across the fields like a teasing laugh.

The gloom which had wanted to coalesce in Mika's soul gradually flew away. She began humming in rhythm to the rushing hooves and even Willy became jovial again, even boisterous.

***

Willy's change had not remained hidden from his madcap friends, yes, they had even learnt of the promise his stepfather, old Exts had extracted from his son-in-law before the engagement – to avoid gaming, clubs, and all extravagant foolishness, and to lead the life of upright men. Since they knew his tendency to hold to his word under all circumstances once given, they diligently avoided getting together with him. Shrugging their shoulders, they called him a "lost man" and did not concern themselves with him anymore.

So Willy could work undisturbed on securing his principles.

Principles! – They eventuate out of the needs of our existence and capture us. But he had accepted them from outside himself through willpower, had thrown them into himself like stones, and was piling them on top of each other to make a wall around his soul. He was walling it in with hard, lifeless rules. Like a stab in the back, abruptly, he had wanted to deliver himself from his past, from his wildly laughing, lightly flitting being. The deeper he came to battle with himself, the harder became his advance. He exchanged an all the more disconsolate split for his unity, and just those quiet, fine notes of his past which he had wanted to chase away with his brow proved to be his hardest adversaries. He ascribed it to their hidden, irrefutable effects that between the scree of his assumed cleverness the colourful spring of distant years sprouted up again and again. Then there was only one path: he had to starve himself, slowly rot away. Under the debris of duties, he first had to swelter and atrophy before he could live, live like he had promised. That's why he blocked all outlets from which the craving could return with torments and ordeals to shake his heart.

He fearfully avoided all deep conversations with his wife. He shunned the stirring sermons of the old pastor in Nesselnitz and only went to church in the far more distant Grabendorf. The cutting daredevilry by which the loud, empty rhetoric of the young pastor there suited him better. They supported his recovery.

With merciless severity, he forced his life into the narrow, sober cycle of the days. He conducted the operations of his estate himself, administered all the books, decided on the cutting of the forests, oversaw the breeding of stock, rummaged in the tack room, and crept about in all the lofts.

His estate manager degenerated into a worker and asked for his release.

Now his activity became a fever, an intoxication. With the dawn, his principles tore him from his bed and drove him down into the yard. With noisy energy he forced everything into a hasty pace, his supervision became an affliction to his employees. He sunk slowly from one abyss into the next: from the whirl of senses into the whirl of soulless principles. For him the commandments of sobriety, industry and faithfulness were nothing but commandments. They were probably seizing him little by little, but like pinching crab's claws.

At the same time, he was neglecting himself, his wife and his mother. In his workday coat with thick high boots, he walked around by himself on Sunday. He was now beginning to hate the music which he had so loved before. When his mother told stories from the days of his youth, he stood up and left the "prattle" hastily.

***

But it came as it had to come.

And it was precisely a quiet note which touched his soul, mishandled by respectability, like a skimming shadow; a seemingly quite trivial accident called up the fate so that it came over him finally and calmly as if he had not battled it with his severity but tended it in loving devotion.

The day had died like a butterfly which spreads the deep delight of all its beauty about itself one more time with the last, tired stirrings of its wings. Rustling winds spun the little leaves and brought them to rest. The trees let their shadows glide down and greenish-grey clouds wandered over, now lining up in the heavens to suck up all the last beauty of the skies.

Willy and Mika were walking in the park, Willy a few steps ahead and armed with a riding crop which he swung from time to time in the bushes to his left so that destroyed leaves tumbled onto the gravel of the path. Mika followed him in the absent-minded manner of a dreaming child.

"See," Mika said to him, "see, the evening is scurrying over the mountains like a big, grey bird; it is still asleep on his resting wing; and now the gentle stars of its eyes are opening."

In answer, the man addressed laughed, short and rough, while he continued striking his crop whistling into the bushes.

"But, Willy, have you become vulgar!", the young woman cried in outrage.

Then he turned around, propped his fists on his sides, and looked down at her disparagingly.

"Mika, it again just concerns one word. What you call poetry, I call ... oh, what's the point!" He broke off and continued his activity with offensive indifference.

But his wife spoke with a trembling, but decisive voice, "Now please, finish at least, otherwise I will go straight to my room."

He turned in astonishment; but then he smiled as if over a child and said bitingly, "I, my revered wife, I call it a daze, laziness, eh! — What to me is the evening with its mild, haha!! Wasn't so with its mild eyes when tomorrow my barley will spoil precisely because of those beautiful, clouded eyes. Let that be! — Tell me rather whether you are satisfied with the new breed of hens."

The look in her eyes which she tossed at him during these words was deeply sad, motionless, and also obtained no friendlier shimmer when Willy wanted to make out that the entire conversation was a teasing cloaked in a serious garb. She felt the shadows of rising tears approaching and left the garden.

Willy did not seek to detain her. He did nothing. After he had pondered to himself for a while, he lifted his head slowly and looked stiffly along the path which Mika had taken from him. Then he ran his trembling hand over his paling forehead and murmured dully always in the same direction, "Now, have I not turned out well, just as you wanted? — Why are you running from me? I have given my mother joy and held to my word of honour just as it ...", here he made a gesture of disgust and twisted his face into a grimace, "... as it behooves one", he concluded and smiled mockingly, painfully.

"Haha! Why this self-torture and oppression of others!?", he continued muttering to himself, "it is no use though. Every life must be one with its will! And what use is the best will when it remains a stranger to the soul! — I see where that is steering ... a sober criminal ... desolation from uprightness ... becoming a thorn, a poison, a worm ... low, broken, cold ... ugh!"

These thoughts which he had already carried around with himself for so long like a burden, he stammered them passionately like the joy of a salvation. Then he sat down on a wooden park bench, propped his elbows on his knees and gazed across the lawn.

He lingered for a long, long time motionless in this position. Sometimes he straightened up, breathed heavily, and gazed towards the solitary light in his house behind the trees which did not want to go out. Then he tore at his body with indignation, a short thorn stabbed him on the way to his home; he wanted to rise up. But each time he had to give up before a repugnance which rose up within himself. Then he struck at his chest and stuttered, "Cursed! — But I can't!"

This silent struggle did not want to end. The night deepened, clouds rose from the forests, slowly and tenaciously, like dirty waters, stood still for a while like gawking balls, to then drift slowly apart like thawing masses of vomit. Under these dreary, formless waves the beautiful endlessness of the deep blue night sky vanished more and more. The last star was extinguished after midnight.

The solitary light up in the house, which had waited so steadfastly for him, scurried helplessly to a few windows and then vanished as well.

Willy rose and murmured to the extinguished light, "In fury and pain, you will now fall asleep; you will rise dismayed, wake with worry, seek painfully to understand, and then ... what comes next nobody knows. But what can I do about it that your conventionality ruins me? — Let me be upright in my foolish, mad simplicity, be one with myself — well — and if not even that, if nothing else works, then to ruin."

Quietly he stole to his own, in that he escaped through the little back gate into the field, and the further away he went, the more did his gait become a victorious, jubilant striding.

When he turned around once, his home had already disappeared and he walked on more hurriedly.

***

They waited a long time on his return.

Comprehensive enquiries were made without any fuss.

Many traces were found, but none led to the goal. They ended on the railroads, at the crossroads, vanished into the city or disappeared on the shore of the sea.

For the house of the General-Director it was a time full of terrible sorrow whose bitterness lay in the secrecy which had to carry it.

The old gentleman thereby preserved a steadfast confidence.

When one morning, however, he received a letter, the security of his quiet hope was destroyed and a furious crease dug itself ever deeper between his brows. Whilst he had usually listened with the patience of an angel to the ever more excessive plans of the ladies for finding the fugitive, and when very astutely detailed measures were discussed had rejected them finally with well-played apprehension, so now an ugly irritability overcame him often with the frequent, long discussions. Then it happened that he struck his knee with a quiet, mocking laugh, stood up, set his shoulders, and without a word of apology went to his room whose door he carefully locked.

There he let himself fall down exhausted in his chair and collapsed. But then he pulled himself together and pulled that letter with trembling hand from his breast pocket.

He ran his fingers over it and investigated it exactly, as if the impossible could occur, that the form of the writing, the colour of the paper, the flecks on the paper, or the stamp could give him a hold for deciphering the secret which this happy and string man had swept away. And that he did not speak the word to which it urged him, the old man reproached himself more and more; but for days he felt it to be enormously calming to take sides with his son-in-law against the suspicions of his own heart. Certainly this resistance became weaker and weaker, and one day, behind closed doors, he had the courage to confess his conviction to himself.

"Yes, what is it to me then", he said to himself, "with the piece of paper, as if I could track down the secret by looking at it! I know that I will learn nothing more about him and am yet so stupid ... so ... so", and he tapped his left index finger contemptuously against his forehead. "There it stands: 'Let the search begin! I went because I could not keep my word. Never to be seen again! Willy.' — That is though enough for old white-haired me and that Hamburg is on the postmark proves nothing. Yes, for what purpose in all the world is all of it, this advising, this deception and arduous nullity of hope before the ladies?! — I will tell you: you were made a fool of by Willy and you are called Exts, old fool, not in vain, for that is out too, out!" —

After he had held this short and forceful lecture, he went resolutely to the women who were still eagerly in discussion, and he explained quite roughly to them that further inquiries after the "lost man" were hopeless, "effectively hopeless", and must stop in consideration for the reputation of the family because their secrecy could not be continued anymore. He had relieved them thereby from the torture of a hopeless situation and wanted to make possible for them the peace of resignation. But what did his man's heart, hardened by a long life, know of the torture which must swing the woman to renounce her love!

Old Mrs Vogt died of these pains.

Mika lapsed into wordless brooding. After some time of sitting around dead, she went to bed with the attitude of a sorely harried game animal, turned her face to the wall and asked with quiet, empty voice, "Take the light away."

The curtains were drawn. The poor being lay motionless in the darkness, and when the curtains moved with the opening and closing of the door so that a sharp beam of sunlight slid through the room, then she groaned as if cut by knives.

She had no illness, but she was sick, deeply sick.

Finally she learnt to walk and speak again. But she had forgotten her smile for ever.

The "Moschen" estate was sold and Mika moved in with her parents.

***

Ten times the winter had strewn white death over the earth, ten times the snow had also buried the flowers of memory in Mika's heart, and the soft and heavy mist of resignation was already beginning to spread over the desolate expanse of her soul when one morning a footman from the "Moschen" estate brought a letter from the new owner. The man dripped with sweat, was breathless with awe and exertion, and vanished hastily after he had placed the letter in the still hand of old Mr Exts. The General-Director's family were just sitting down to breakfast.

Not expecting anything, the old gentleman opened the letter. A dirty playing card fell out. Mika stooped down to pick it up. At the same time she threw a curious look at it.

Her face immediately lost all its colour, her eyes widened as if an invisible hand had placed a noose around her throat. But no sound came over her lips. Carefully she turned the card up and down as though she was looking for something on it.

Finally she held the card away from herself and strained to look at it. With that she smiled softly, happily, and murmured with deep breaths, "Finally, finally, finally ... now I can bury you."

The General-Director's hand sunk limply with the letter onto the armrest. He cries mutely, "Oh no, not that ... hung ... a vagabond ... hung in his garden!"

Mika springs up and hurries out. They want to stop her, but it is no use. In a few minutes, she is striding with flying haste on the familiar path to her former home.

The old gentleman has the carriage harnessed and goes after her. He overtakes her midway and pulls her into the carriage.

"Poor Mika", he says and wants to take her in his arms. But she fiercely detachs herself and only ever looks with burning, rigid eyes into the distance where the rooves of the estate buildings rise up.

"Faster, faster!", she gasps, and the carriage hastens there as though it is flying.

Finally they are there.

"Where is he?", she asks trembling.

The owner points to the garden and Mika runs ahead of everyone.

When the men arrive at the place of sorrow, they see a woman kneeling upright before the body.

Is that Mika?

Her hands waving downwards spasmodically, her face rigid and deeply furrowed, and her eyes lying dead in their cavities like grey stones.

Nothing betrays that she is living. She is as motionless as the body of the ragged vagabond on the bench before her.

Now she reaches into her bodice, pulls out the smeared card, and begins to read with a cruel voice,

"Home was my heaven. Paradise still has a branch for me. I will soon hang from it, a rotten, bad fruit. But I saw an angel before I died, it was you, Mika. Farewell, forgive me where there is something to forgive. For I was a man. — Your Willy."

She sings the last words with a jubilant strong voice, the words carried as though in eulogy.

"Child, dear child! — Mika!", the General-Director begs and embraces her arms.

She does not hear.

She just sings in the madness of her jubilation. In between she laughs happily and makes motions of flying.

An Excerpt from *My Life*

Meanwhile my external life circumstances were knotted up almost to insufferability, and because all applications for a different [teaching] position remained without success, I forced myself with even more obstinacy to free the shackles by means of my writerly talents. I turned away from writing poems and undertook to portray through two stories the secrets of human life that experience and observation had taught me. I sent my neatly written manuscript to the publisher of whom I knew nothing other than that Gerhart Hauptmann brought his books out there. I sent it in May 1896. Five agonising months passed. The longer a reply was not forthcoming, the more I hoped for nothing out of fear and dared not write a reminder, so as not to entirely destroy the increasingly fading chimera. In this greatest inner hardship, I received a letter which notified me in such commending, even admiring expressions of the book's acceptance, that, thrown out of the depths and the blackest night into the heights and into the light, after skimming the first words, I was unable to speak for happiness, left the room because I feared the house would fall down, and went down to the schoolyard under the clear autumn skies where I read to the end the writing which was bringing me, the haunted, lifelong prisoner, into freedom, honour and sunshine and giving me proper self-belief. Since that hour I know that happiness can shock as much as pain, as the world turned before my eyes, the skies danced above me and only after half an hour was I able to speak again coherently and comprehensibly to those around me who had really begun to believe that I had gone mad. [...]

I also want to mention the complaint to the Ministry over my "blasphemous, immoral book" by a Theology Professor at the University of Breslau, and his desire for official sanctions against the author. Only in passing should the case be brought to mind which a man of the district brought against me for libel, since he felt associated with the main character of the story "Meicke, the Devil", abetted by one of my disloyal friends, supported by the academics and helped actively by my colleagues, who all burned to ruin the uncomfortable one who had now dared, to the indignation and bewilderment of all right-minded people, to stretch his hand out for the author's laurels. I was convicted in the first and the second case. But disgusted by this incessant war against malicious enemies, having beaten my sickness and recovered, at the same time shaken by the death of another child, I experienced all this jostling like something estranged and remained true to the intention of drawing my strength from this combative life struggle and aiming at the lofty goal of my literary work. During the ever increasing hollowing out of my body through sickness, I wrote in one year the novella "The Shingle Maker" and the three novels "Leonore Griebel", "Three Nights" and "The Buried God". With that I saw the gates to recognition coming loose, though they still lay far-off in indistinctly foreseeable parts whose light was nevertheless embracing me so that I began to march towards them.

About the Publisher

Our mission is to provide translations into English of the complete works of neglected major European writers. We do not cherry-pick works that seem the most marketable, but rather seek to provide a complete collection of each writer's works so that readers can follow the writer's development and decide on its merits for themselves.